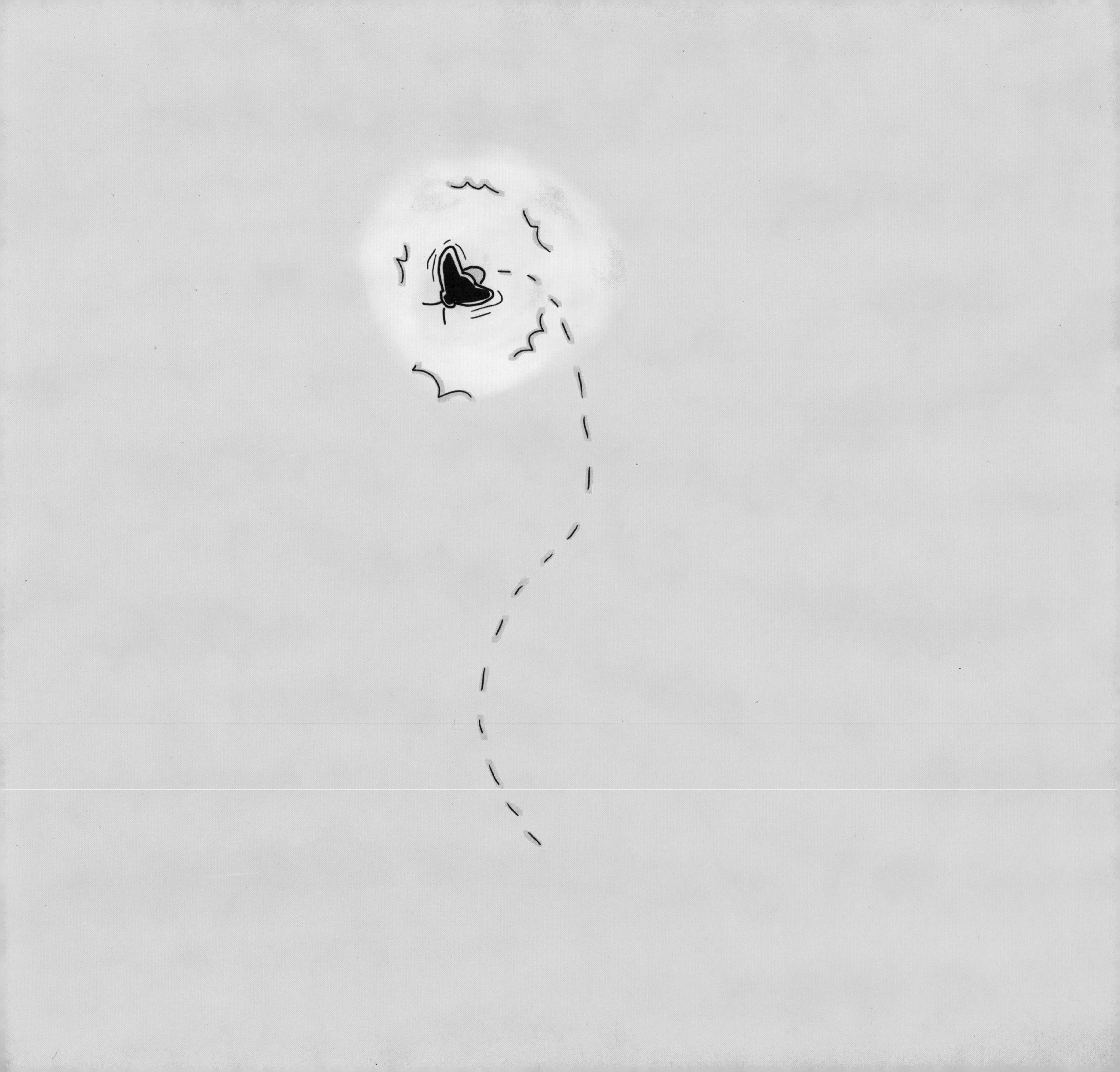

Missing Daddy

Mariame Kaba

Illustrated by
bria royal

Haymarket Books
Chicago, Illinois

Published in 2019 by Haymarket Books
P.O. Box 180165, Chicago, IL 60618
www.haymarketbooks.org

ISBN: 978-1-64259-036-4

Distributed by Consortium Book Sales and Distribution.

Cover artwork by Bria M. Royal. Book design by Jamie Kerry and Bria M. Royal.

Printed in Canada by union labor.

Library of Congress Cataloging-in-Publication data is available.

10 9 8 7 6 5 4 3 2 1

"Each and every family is unique.
From its people, to its food, to the words
That we speak.
Related or chosen, large or small,
We can feel loved, even when the world puts up a wall."

—Jane Ball

Daddy calls me light bug
because I’m so pretty and bright.

Since I don’t see him very much,
I hold onto his words real tight.

Daddy went away to prison
when I was only three.

When I ask my grandma why he's there,
she says, "Baby, the reasons are many."

Sometimes my classmates
laugh and make fun.

They say, “You know, your daddy’s
a criminal so that makes you one.”

I guess some kids forget that
words can really hurt your feelings.

Grandma says everyone should be kinder
and choose words that are gentle and healing.

I try to be brave and
hold back my heavy tears.

I feel a blue wave of sadness.
My daddy won’t be home for years.

Mama works day and night.
She's always on her feet.

I miss her, but she says,
"Baby, you know we have to eat."

My teacher, Ms. Lee, taught us that
there are all kinds of families.
Some kids only have a mommy
or others two daddies.

Those who love us help us grow,
no matter who they are.
They are our true family,
whether near or far.

I have an older sister named Mary
who I never get to see.
She lives with her mommy
in a place called DC.

I wish we could talk regularly,
'cause we share the same story.
I want to tell her that I miss Daddy,
but I don't want her to worry.

At school, I talk to the counselor, Ms. Parker.
I guess it helps me feel a little bit better.

She asks me a lot of questions
about my daddy in prison.
Sometimes I don’t want to speak,
so I talk about my ballet lesson.

When visiting day is near,
I can hardly sleep.

I’m so excited, the happiness
in my soul is deep.

11:11

We travel to the prison.
It is far, far away.

Getting there takes
Grandma and me all day.

Finally, I see Daddy across
the visiting room.

His laugh to me is like fireworks, a
loud, colorful boom.

I run and jump into his arms
and he hugs me tight.

“Good to see you my little light
bug, always so pretty and bright.”

The end.

Author's Note

I wrote this book out of frustration. In my anti-prison work, I've witnessed firsthand the ravages of incarceration and its impact(s) on our communities. Over the years, I've often been asked by caregivers, educators, and organizers for resources to help children with an incarcerated loved one to cope with loss, grief, and trauma. I've struggled to come up with good resources to share so I decided to create one myself.

There are 2.7 million children under 18 who have an incarcerated parent and over 5 million have experienced the incarceration of a parent at some point in their lives. In other words, 1 in 28 American children (3.6%) have an incarcerated parent. Thirty years ago, the number was 1 in 125. About 1 in 9 Black children and 1 in 28 Latino children have an incarcerated parent. More than 14,000 children of incarcerated parents enter foster care each year.

These numbers are staggering. As a result of the epidemic of incarceration, millions of children have endured traumatic separations from their parents. This has impacted their material conditions, their mental health, their school performance, and their overall well-being.

Each of these children has a story to tell, yet we rarely hear their voices in public. Many children cannot articulate their feelings of longing for their incarcerated parent and so they keep their anger, sadness, and fear bottled up. This book is my attempt to amplify the voices of children with incarcerated loved ones.

I am deeply appreciative and grateful to bria m. royal for their gorgeous illustrations which brought the story to life. I am also profoundly thankful to Jane Ball whose thoughtful edits helped the main character find her authentic voice. Thanks, too, to Hana Worku who came up with just the right words at the right time. Thanks also to Angie Manfredi, Eve L. Ewing, Kelly Hayes, Mandi Hinkley, Maya Schenwar, and Santera Michels for reading drafts of this story and offering critical feedback.

Finally, this book is dedicated to all of the children who miss their loved ones because of a cruel punishment system that does little to make our communities safer.

—MK

Discussion Guide

1. Notice the variety of feelings the main character has throughout the story. Can you name some of them? Do you think it's possible to still feel joyful when you're dealing with a challenge? How do you find moments of happiness in a challenging/difficult situation? What strategies do you use to cope with these challenging moments?

2. What do you think Grandma meant by "the reasons are many," in response to the main character's question?

3. Why do you think that Mama has to work all day and night?

4. The main character doesn't reach out to her sister because she's afraid she'll make her worry. Can you relate to this feeling? What would encourage you or prevent you from reaching out to someone who shares your story?

5. What can you do if you notice someone saying hurtful things to others? How can you support your friend/peer who are being bullied? How can you support your friend/peer who is bullying?

6. Where is the main character's father? Do you know what jail or prison is? Who goes there? Why do people go there? How can you support and help a friend who might have a parent or loved one in jail or prison?

7. Which friends or family members do you go to when you have a problem or a worry? Why do you choose to go to them? Is there anyone at school that you could reach out to? Why or why not?

About the Author: Mariame Kaba

Mariame Kaba is an educator and organizer based in New York City. She has been active in the anti-criminalization and anti-violence movements for the past 30 years. Mariame is the founder and director of Project NIA, a grassroots organization with a long-term vision to end youth incarceration.

Learn more at www.mariamekaba.com

About the Illustrator: Bria Royal

Bria Royal is a multidisciplinary artist from Chicago, IL. She considers her animation, comics, paintings and zines to be the result of a radical healing process that she hopes others will benefit from seeing unfold. Much of her work centralizes black and brown imaginations of womxnhood, femininity and gender fluidity through a lens of ecofeminism, Afro-futurism and contemporary mythology.

Learn more at briaroyal.com

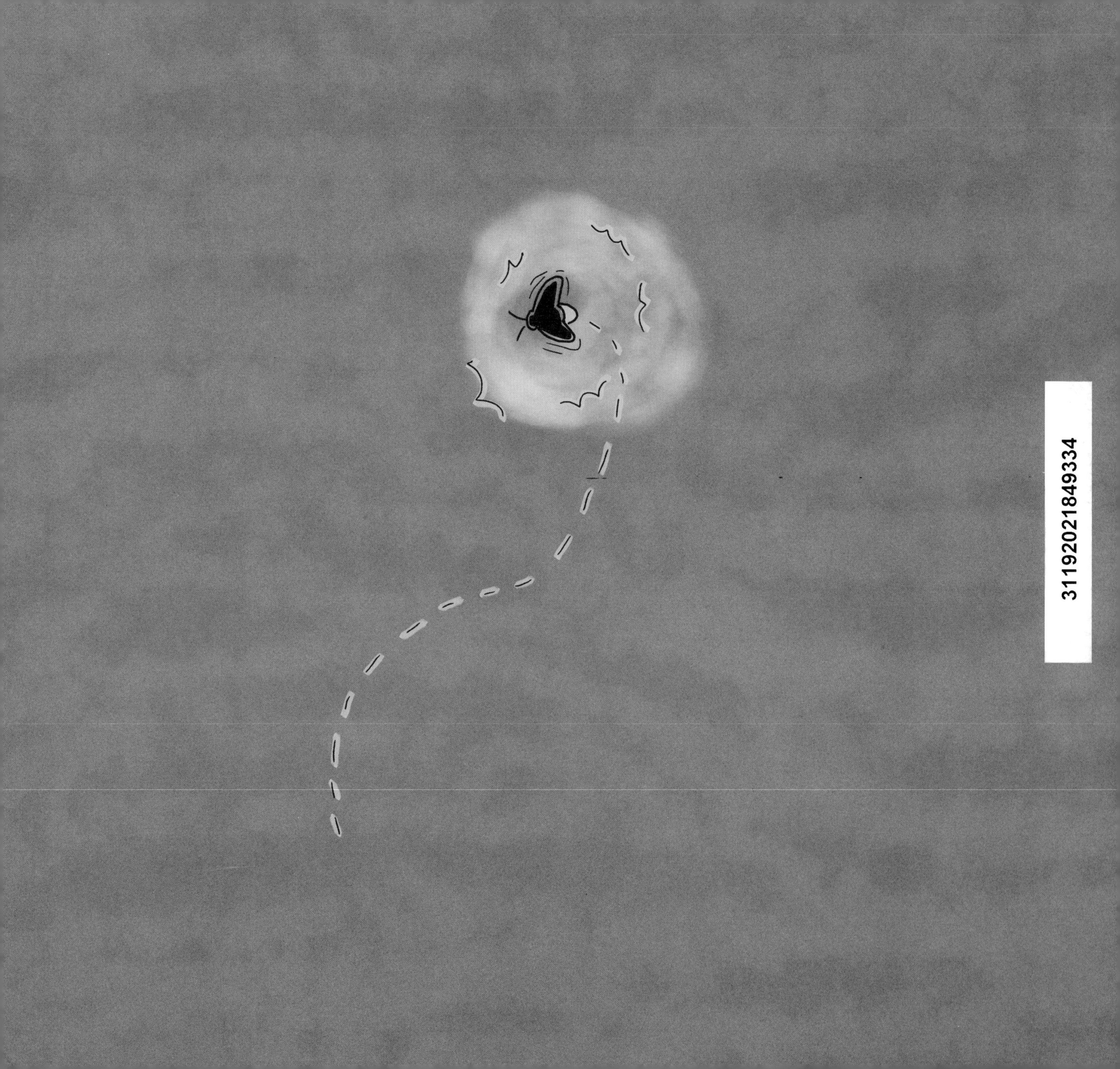